SEPT-OPUS

Jyotin Goel is a feature film and television writer and director based in Mumbai. He wrote and directed the animated children's film, *Bird Idol*, for Warner Bros. This is his first book for children.

Rajiv Eipe studied Fine Arts at Sir J.J. School of Art, Mumbai; and Animation Film Design at the National Institute of Design, Ahmedabad. He currently lives in Bangalore and spends his time doing animation and illustration projects.

SEPT-OPUS

Adventures of
an Almost-Octopus

JYOTIN GOEL
Illustrated by RAJIV EIPE

RED TURTLE

RUPA

For Rehaan,
the sunshine in our day.

Published in Red Turtle by
Rupa Publications India Pvt. Ltd 2015
7/16, Ansari Road, Daryaganj
New Delhi 110002

Sales Centres:
Allahabad Bengaluru Chennai
Hyderabad Jaipur Kathmandu
Kolkata Mumbai

Copyright © Jyotin Goel 2015
Illustrations copyright © Rupa Publications India Pvt. Ltd 2015

This is a work of fiction. Names, characters, places and incidents
are either the product of the author's imagination or are used
fictitiously and any resemblance to any actual person,
living or dead, events or locales is entirely coincidental.

ISBN: 978-81-291-3592-6

First impression 2015

10 9 8 7 6 5 4 3 2 1

The moral right of the author has been asserted.

I

'And now, ladies and gentlemen, boys and girls,' the announcer boomed, 'for the Final, Fantastical Act of the Goa Sea World show, preeeesentinggg the Cleverest Creatures in the sea—the Octopi!'

That announcement had two mistakes. As every octopus knows, the plural of 'octopus' is 'octopuses', not 'octopi' (Octopi is the language octopuses speak). The second mistake was calling octopuses 'the cleverest creatures in the sea'—they're NOT. They're the cleverest anywhere! For instance, which other creature (including humans) can do what the octopuses did in the next fifteen minutes of the show? A trapeze act with two octopus catchers twirling *six* octopus flyers through the air! A football match, which was

actually a *four*-ball match—four balls in play at the same time! And topping it all, not an orchestra but an *oct*-estra: four octopuses playing as a sixteen-piece band. Awesome!

The show ended to thunderous applause. And, even when clapping, octopus spectators outdid human spectators. For while humans with their two hands went 'clap', the eight-limbed octopuses went 'clap-clap-clap-clap'! In the audience, Irrig cheered and Medit whooped and Infl whistled and… What? Why such strange names? Because they're octopuses, that's why! Since eight is a very important number among octopuses, all octo-names end in '8'. So Irrig's name is really Irrig8, Medit is Medit8, Infl is Infl8 and so on. And as they're the cleverest creatures on earth, they just drop the '8' and save time. Anyway:

- ∾ Overw went 'clap-clap-clap-clap'
- ∾ Imit went 'clap-clap-clap-clap'
- ∾ Rot went 'clap-clap-clap-swish'
- ∾ Tool went…

Wait a minute! 'Clap-clap-clap-*swish*'? What's that 'swish' about? Oh, that's our hero, Rot. One of his tentacles never grew more than halfway so when he claps, his seventh limb doesn't meet the short eighth limb. Naturally, his fourth clap simply goes 'swish' (or sometimes 'floosh' if he gets too excited). Of course, this is just his everyday identity. Secretly, though, he's a superhero who stops crime, fights evildoers, saves the world and does other cool stuff. But I was telling you about the others who were cheering and applauding. Now let's see, there was... Oh? You want to know more about Rot? About his adventures and secret identity and his special limb? You're sure about this? Well, if you insist, here goes:

A seven-limbed octopus called Rot,
Never in his wildest dreams thought
He'd be more than a zero,
But he turned out a hero,
So let me tell you how Rot got hot!

It all began when various water creatures were transported from an aquarium in Mumbai to the spanking new Goa Sea World. There, the Sea World handlers unloaded tanks teeming with sea life. There were the biggies—the killer whales and the sharks; the crowd pullers—dolphins, seals and penguins; the 'us-es'—walruses, platypuses and octopuses. And, of course, there were the little ones of all species. The handlers had to be especially cautious with the youngsters because many of them were yet to hatch—hundreds of eggs that had to be handled *very* carefully, as if they were, well, eggs! Unfortunately, one of the handlers was Claude Custado, or Clumsy Claude. If there was a stone on the ground, Claude *would* trip over it; if there was a slippery tile, Claude *would* slip; if there was a stiff door, Claude *would* catch his fingers in the jamb. No one in his right mind would ask Claude to unload and carry eggs. So, naturally, someone did! Claude, however, surprised everyone. He skipped past the stone, skirted the slippery tile, sauntered through the laboratory's stiff door and... (pick one of the following)

1. ...carefully placed the octopus-egg tray on the lab table
2. ...gently slid the octopus-egg tray onto the lab table
3. ...PLONKED the octopus-egg tray on the lab table

If you picked (1), you don't know Claude. If you picked (2), the story ends here and you may as well stop reading. If you picked (3), you're right but you get no prize because who said anything about prizes?

Anyway, this is what happened next: the eggs thumped and jumped and one broke loose from its string (octopus eggs are attached together with strings of jelly) and rolled towards the table edge. Claude grabbed at it wildly, but all he ended up with was air as the egg danced and spun right off the table!

Claude, though, was Goan and every Goan is a born footballer. With a frantic twist, Claude stuck his leg under the falling egg. The egg landed right on Claude's shoe, stopped there for a moment as if holding its breath, and then lazily rolled off, falling to the ground. Hurriedly, Claude stooped to gather up the tiny egg. He lifted it up and examined it. It was fine, intact, perfect, not a scratch. Scarcely believing his luck, Claude looked around. No one there— no one had seen the accident. Quickly, he reached into his pocket and pulled out a tube of superglue. (Since he broke things so often, Claude always carried superglue in his pocket. He had also very often glued his pockets shut!) He squirted glue onto the egg and stuck it back to the string. Shoving the uncapped superglue tube back into his trouser pocket, Claude looked around—still no one. He slunk out of the door, trying not to appear guilty, whistling a nervous tune, casually attempting to stick his hands into his pockets. For some reason, his right hand wouldn't go into the pocket. When last seen, Claude was walking rapidly away, his right hand repeatedly sliding off his jeans. A few minutes later, other handlers entered the lab, placed the seemingly undisturbed egg trays in machines called incubators and left the eggs to hatch in their own time.

Two weeks later, the eggs hatched. Unlike bird eggs, octopus eggs don't crack open—they go all gooey and messy and the hatchlings slither out of the slime. As the babies emerged, the handlers gathered them up and quickly took them to their natural home—water. One baby, however, appeared strangely reluctant to move along. A handler noticed and picked it up gently. What the handler didn't see was that this particular baby had one limb that was shorter than his other limbs. For this is what had happened: Clumsy Claude's superglue had seeped into the egg and attached itself to a limb of the baby, not letting it grow normally. When the baby emerged from its egg and stretched its cramped limbs, one limb was all doubled up, unfolding to just half the length of the others. As the baby looked curiously at this unique limb, the handler scooped it up, put it into a water bag with all the other octopuses and carried it away.

2

In very little time, the baby grew up and became a one-foot-tall, orange-pink teenager called Rot. Now why would Rot's Mom (Delic8) and Dad (Clarin8) name their son 'Rot'? Well, they didn't. They had named him 'Equ8' because they felt that despite his halfway limb, he was any other octopus' equal. However, that name didn't last long. The reason was this: octopuses move by using their limbs to push against the water, much like a boat's oars. But if a boat has four oars on one side and three on the other, it would turn right around! And that's exactly what happened to little Equ8. One day, as he swam behind his parents, his brother Pyr8 and sister Gyr8, he suddenly spun around and started swimming in the opposite direction. Delic spotted him right away.

'Equ! Where are you going?' she called.

She swam back quickly and turned him around. Another time, as the family scrambled toward the food being poured out by the Sea World keepers, Clarin noticed Equ heading away from the food.

'What's the matter, my lad?' asked Clarin, swimming up to him. 'Not hungry?'

Equ looked confused. Gently, Clarin turned him around and led him back to the food. But this was a worry. Delic and Clarin looked at each other. Perhaps a doctor would know what to do?

∽

'Hmm,' said the doctor, as he examined Equ's halfway limb. 'Problimb.'

Delic and Clarin looked at each other again, puzzled.

'P...prob*limb*?' asked Delic.

'Problimb,' said the doctor.

The *problem* was that the doctor was a blowfish, not an octopus. And just as octopuses speak 'Octopi', blowfish speak 'Blowish'. The only way octopuses and blowfish can understand each other is by speaking the common water creature language, 'Fishy'. There's just one hitch, however. No one speaks Fishy well.

'Big problimb,' said Dr Blowhard.

'No, no,' said Clarin, pointing at Equ's little limb. 'Small problimb.'

'Yes, yes,' agreed Dr Blowhard. 'Small problimb *is* big problimb.'

'Can do help, doctor?' asked Delic.

'Yes, yes,' said Dr Blowhard, yanking out some seaweed, chewing it to pulp and spitting it on to Equ's 'problimb'. 'Seaweed good for limb. "Genus Broken-

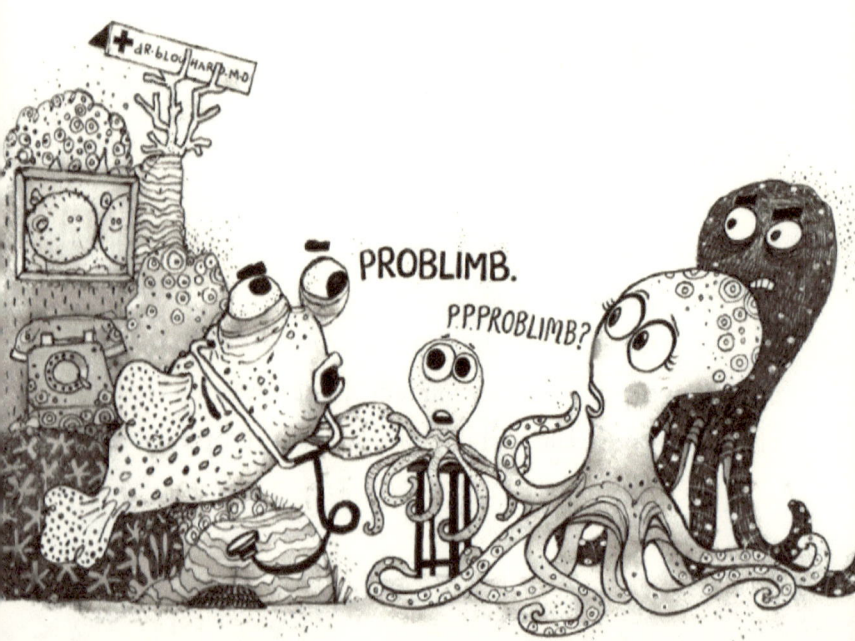

bonus".'

'Do you think it will work?' Delic asked Clarin anxiously, as they left the clinic.

'"Genus Broken-bonus"? Broken-*bogus* more likely!' said Clarin. 'That doctor always sounded fishy to me! Don't worry, I'm sure as he gets bigger, Equ's limb will grow out.'

But Equ's 'problimb' didn't grow out and, as he continued to spin around at the most unexpected moments, his classmates couldn't help but laugh at him. Once, during Sports Day in Junior School, the octopuses were participating in a fifteen-legged race. Octopuses are particularly fond of this type of race where the leg of one octopus is tied to the leg of another and they run together on their 'fifteen' legs. Equ and his brother, Pyr, were moving together perfectly and actually leading. Unfortunately, Equ got so excited that he forgot to concentrate and spun right around, ending up back-to-back with Pyr.

'Ha ha! Look at that!' guffawed Irrit8.

'Equ's spun around again!' chuckled Overw8.

And that was the cue for the class wit, Po8, to come up with a limerick:

There's this octopus with a funny trait,
He can't, won't, doesn't go straight,
Doesn't know when he's spun,
Has he ended or begun?
It's all the same to our buddy, Rot-8!

The class yelled with laughter and the name just stuck. Even when Equ grew into a teenager and had managed to control his spinning (except when he forgot about not getting excited while running), no one called him anything but 'Rot' (as usual, the '8' had been dropped).

Rot, though, was made of stern stuff. He was not going to let anything stop him. The more they laughed, the more determined he became.

'I'll get into the trapeze act!' he said to himself. 'That'll show them! Tumboo'll help me practise!'

'Tumboo' means 'tent' in Hindi but Tumboo wasn't a tent, of course. She was a turtle, a teenager like Rot, and Rot's best friend. It was just that she was a little too fond of eating and now looked like an over-stuffed canvas bag.

'Trapeze?' Tumboo said to Rot, looking down at

him from the upper ledge of the artificial reef that was their school building. (She spoke Turtle-tongue, the turtle language that Rot also spoke, having learnt it from Tumboo.) 'Of course, I'll help.' Tumboo heaved herself off the shelf, straight at Rot. 'Catch!' she shouted.

'Yaaaah!!' Rot yelled, seeing her plunge towards him like a ship's anchor.

SPLATTTT! Tumboo's bulk squished Rot like a swatted bug.

'Hmm,' Tumboo said, looking at the flattened Rot. 'Obviously, you're not a Catcher. Maybe a Flyer?'

'M…maybe…' Rot wheezed from somewhere underneath.

Perhaps he *could* be a Flyer, thought Rot. After all, if someone flung him through the air, he couldn't very well turn around. So there he was at the trapeze try-outs, twirling through the air, listening to Tumboo's cheers. Unluckily for Rot, he reached the Catcher in mid-twirl, exactly at the point where his halfway limb was front and centre. The Catcher clutched but there was nothing there. Rot flew past the Catcher, missed the pool altogether and landed SPLOTTT! on the

hard poolside floor!

'Nope,' Tumboo said, scraping Rot off the tiles. 'Not a Flyer, either.'

Rot tried four-ball next. However, having a halfway limb isn't very helpful when there are four balls flying around. Balls kept hitting Rot's head, even when he wasn't trying to head them! As the balls pounded him from every direction, Rot thought, 'Maybe I should try out (Ow!) for the oct-estra. At least (Ouch!) music doesn't hurt anyone. So I'll play three instruments (Oof!) instead of four. It's quality (Aah!) that counts, not quantity (Ugh!).'

The oct-estra was the biggest attraction at Goa Sea World. Humans came from all over the world to listen to the performing octopuses. All the other water creatures, the performing seals and dolphins, the killer whales and sharks, knew that this one act put the octopuses on top. Conscious of their special status, the octopuses were determined to have their very best musicians play the sixteen instruments. And who were the best? Why, Rot's own family, of course—Delic8, Clarin8, Gyr8. The fourth, Rot's old uncle Quart8, had just announced his retirement. But there was no competition for his position. It was well known in octopus circles that no one could match Rot's family's talent. Rot knew that his family's musical vein ran rich in him. He was bound to get in, despite the missing fourth instrument. Excitedly (but not so excitedly that he rotated), Rot headed for the cove where his family practised. But just as he was rounding the corner, he stopped. Rot's brother, Pyr, was with his parents, talking eagerly to them. Quietly moving closer, Rot listened.

'You really think so, Dad? Mom?' Pyr said. 'You think I'm ready?'

'Yes, dear,' Delic said, 'you are. No other octopus plays as well as you do.'

'Except Rot,' Pyr said, loyally.

'Yes, son,' Clarin said. 'He does, but…'

'But…' echoed Delic.

Just then, Rot swam out from behind the seaweed, smiling brightly. 'Hi, Mom, Dad! Hey, Pyr, did you hear? Uncle Quart's retiring. Now you can get into the oct-estra!'

Clarin shuffled, uneasily. 'Well, son…'

'But what about you, Rot?' Pyr said. 'You're even better than me!'

'That's a laugh, Pyr! You know I can't play four-at-once!'

'But…'

'No buts!' Rot said. 'It's your turn! Right, Dad? Mom?'

Clarin hesitated. 'Um…'

Delic moved forward and put four arms around Rot and four around Pyr. 'You're right, son. It *is* Pyr's turn. Isn't that wonderful?'

'Terrific!' Rot said, thumping Pyr on the back. Pyr grinned bashfully.

'Now let's get Gyr,' Delic said, 'and go out and celebrate!'

'Celebr8?' Rot groaned. 'Must we take that old bore along?'

They laughed and swam off happily.

3

S ome time later, in a lonely corner of Sea World, soft drumbeats sounded from a coral reef. Rot sat on an outcropping, above the water surface seven sticks clutched in his tentacles, slowly drumming on the coral. It was a soft, sad rhythm, but then suddenly Rot seemed to get energized. He drummed faster and faster and finished with a flourish. He raised the sticks in the air and looked around at the empty spectators' galleries.

'Thank you, thank you,' said Rot, acknowledging the cheers of the imaginary crowd. After a moment, he lowered the sticks with a sigh. 'Who said music doesn't hurt?' he mumbled. Abruptly, he threw the sticks over the reef as far as he could.

'Ow!' Tumboo's voice floated over the water. 'Who's

flinging sticks about? Is that you, Rot?'

'Oh no,' Rot muttered. He didn't want company, not now! Scuttling quickly along the coral reef, Rot froze in place. An octopus has a remarkable ability to disguise itself. In fact, even chameleons can't compare with an octopus' powers to change its appearance. In a flash, Rot had altered the colour and texture of his skin to match the coral. He blended in completely, invisible to any passer-by.

'Rot! Where are you?' Tumboo shouted. 'He's never around when you want him,' puffed Tumboo, out of breath as usual. 'Rot!' Tumboo scrambled on to the reef and settled down with a sigh.

'Ow! Gerroff me!' Rot yelled.

Startled, Tumboo looked down. Right under her,

flattened by her weight, was a very coral-like Rot.

'Ah! There you are, Rot,' said Tumboo. 'What're you doing down there?'

'Being squashed by you! Will you GERROFF?!'

'Oh, sorry,' Tumboo said, as she lumbered aside.

Rot, who had been almost plastered to the coral surface, detached himself painfully.

'Why're you doing coral impressions?' Tumboo asked. 'Who're you hiding from?'

'I just (*haahh-hahhh*) wanted to be alone,' Rot replied, gasping for breath. 'Look, I need to breathe. Let's get (*haahh*) into the water and then talk!' (Octopuses have to get back into water within five minutes. They wouldn't last more than that in the open air.)

They slithered into the water. Rot felt it pass through his gills and took a deep breath.

'Ah, that's better! Now what d'you want, Tumboo? Why're you looking for me?'

Tumboo, who was also forgetful, scratched her head with her flipper.

'It was something important. Let's see…'

'Anyway, it's probably time to get back,' Rot said.

'Yeah,' Tumboo said, 'it's mealtime.'

Together, they started swimming towards the gate that separated the reef pool from the main pool of Sea World. They soon reached the dividing wall.

'Shouldn't the gate to the main pool be here?' Tumboo wondered.

'You're right! Where's it gone?'

Rot looked around and started swimming upwards. He swam right to the top, breaking the surface of the water and emerging into the air. Tumboo popped out next to him. Turning right and left, they looked everywhere, but still couldn't spot the gate. Then Rot looked up.

'There it is!' he shouted, pointing to the gate six feet above the water surface.

'But why is it up there?' Tumboo asked. 'And it's getting upper!' she squeaked, forgetting her grammar, as the gate rose even further.

'It's not getting upper, we're going downer!' Rot exclaimed. 'The water level's dropping!'

'Water l...level?' Tumboo stuttered. She slapped her head with her flipper. 'The important thing I had to tell you? Just remembered what it was! They're draining this area today to clean it!'

'What? But they're supposed to make sure all the water creatures are out of the area before draining it!'

Which is exactly what any Sea World worker would have done *except* Claude Custado, who had been entrusted with this seemingly simple task. Clumsy Claude had completely forgotten to check the pool for water creatures before opening the drains. Now he sat at the pool-edge, headphones on, listening to music, happily watching the water level fall.

Water was rapidly gurgling down the gaping mouth of the drain.

'Help!' Tumboo yelled.

'Help!' Rot shouted.

But there was no one to hear them. They struggled against the tug of the water, knowing that if they didn't break free they'd be sucked into the yawning drain. Rot managed to snag a reef-edge with one of his tentacles. He grabbed Tumboo's flipper as she tumbled by and held on desperately.

'Hang on, Tumboo!' Rot gasped.

But the water kept draining away and was now churning like a whirlpool around them. The force

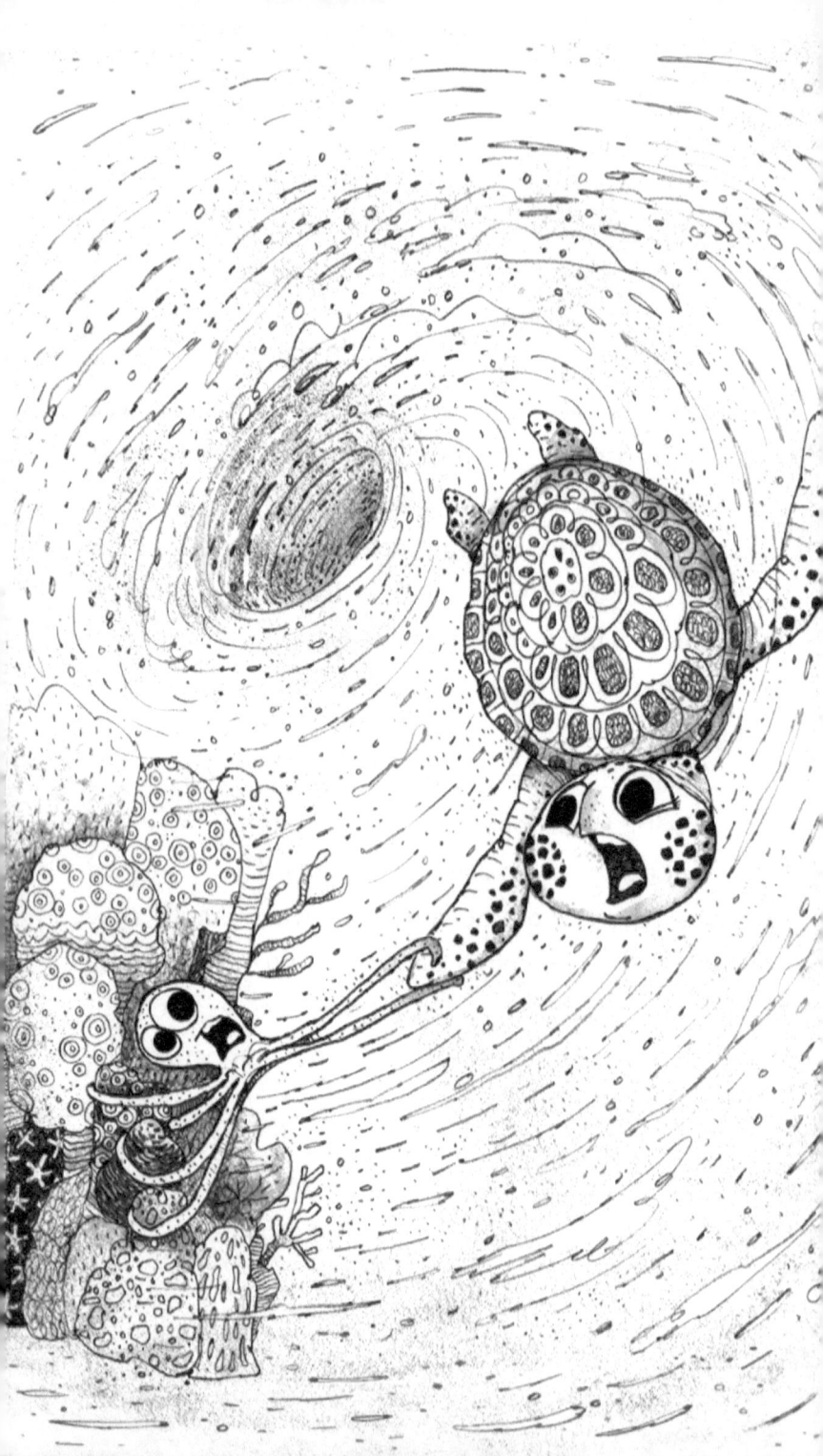

of the water and Tumboo's weight were proving too much for Rot. He could feel his tentacles slipping off the water-slicked reef as he fought to hold on to Tumboo.

'Leave me!' Tumboo shouted. 'Let go! You'll be pulled in, too!'

'Not if I can help it!' Rot hissed through his gritted beak.

But the whirling water was too strong. All at once, Rot's tentacles were yanked off the reef and the two friends went tumbling through the water. Spinning down, Rot reached the drain first. Frantically, he spread his tentacles to the edges of the drain's mouth, keeping himself outside it as the water surged past him. He thought he'd make it, but just then Tumboo, dropping like a rock, loomed over him and her hard shell crashed into Rot.

'Oof!' Rot gasped and his tentacles slipped.

He shot into the drain and vanished into the dark depths below. Tumboo, though, was too wide to get sucked in. Her shell stuck halfway in the drain's mouth and she kept spinning around on her back, rotating like her friend Rot.

At the pool-edge, Clumsy Claude saw the last of the water drain out. Suddenly, he noticed something round and grey-green spinning at the mouth of the drain.

'Hey, wha's dat?' said the surprised Claude. He clambered down the pool ladder to the floor and ambled closer. All at once, he realized what it was—a turtle on its back. Now that all the water had drained out, Tumboo had stopped spinning, but she couldn't get upright again. Helplessly, she lay on her back, her shell halfway in the drain, her flippers waving in the air.

'Oops!' said Clumsy, abruptly remembering that he was supposed to have emptied the area of water creatures before draining it. He looked around—no one seemed to have noticed. He picked up the turtle and hurried to the ladder, hoping to slip her into the main pool before anyone saw him.

By this time, Tumboo was wild with worry.

'Listen to me!' she shouted at Clumsy. 'We've got to save Rot! He's been sucked into the drain!'

But Clumsy didn't speak Turtle-tongue and, ignoring Tumboo, started climbing the ladder.

Tumboo had to do something, anything, to get this man's attention. He was holding her upside down, carrying her away from Rot. An idea popped into her head. She opened her mouth and nipped Clumsy's bottom hard.

'Ow!' Clumsy yelled and dropped Tumboo.

Tumboo plunged towards the pool floor but she knew what to do. Quickly, she pulled her head and flippers back into her shell. She struck the floor with a loud bang that echoed around the empty pool. Tumboo's head and flippers popped out again. Her shell was intact and she was unharmed *except* that she was flat on her back.

'Oh, no!' Tumboo groaned, her flippers flapping helplessly. 'Not again!'

'What was that noise?'

A female human voice sounded from above. Both Clumsy and Tumboo looked up. A pretty human head appeared at the pool-edge, peering down.

'Oops!' went Clumsy (his favourite word). He knew he was in trouble, for this was Dr Reena Renaldo, the official Sea World vet, in charge of the health of all Sea World creatures.

'Is that a turtle?' Reena demanded. She quickly climbed down the ladder. 'What's it doing here? Didn't you check that all the creatures were out before draining the water?'

'Uh…boss…I…I…' Clumsy stammered.

Reena rushed to Tumboo who was flailing her flippers about, trying to roll upright.

'Okay, okay, you'll be all right,' Reena said soothingly to Tumboo. 'Let's see if you're hurt.'

She turned Tumboo upright. Immediately, Tumboo started running towards the drain in the centre of the empty pool (a running turtle isn't very fast).

'Rot! Rot!' Tumboo shouted, lumbering forward as quickly as she could go. 'I'm coming! Try to hang in there!'

Reena tried to pick Tumboo up, but Tumboo squirmed violently, shouting, 'Let me go! Rot's down there! I've got to save him!'

Of course, this was in Turtle-tongue so it wasn't likely that Reena could understand her.

'Easy, easy there,' Reena said. 'I know you fell. We'll just check if you're okay…'

But all Tumboo could hear Reena saying was 'Eeooshivie, eeooshivie, noayuffayllie chekkiifayyy oakayyoo!' for human speech sounds like gobbledygook to all other creatures.

Tumboo continued trying to squirm out of Reena's arms and even snapped at Reena. She put her down gently. At once, Tumboo started moving towards the drain.

'Hmm,' Reena thought. 'She keeps heading for that drain. I wonder if one of the creatures has been sucked in!'

Tumboo saw Reena bending down close to her, pointing towards the drain, asking, 'Frendazoo flushoolapaloo?'

'Rot! Rot!' Tumboo replied, running as fast as she could. 'Octopus! He's down there!'

'Down there' was exactly where Rot was. After Tumboo had crashed into him and knocked him into the drain, Rot had been sucked deeper and deeper into the drainage pipe that connected all Sea World pools to the open sea. Rot thrashed his tentacles about, trying to break free of the current that was pulling him along, but the flow was too strong. He tumbled and turned as he sped down the pipe. Rot knew that once he was ejected into the sea, there was no way he could ever come back. The Sea World keepers would never be able to find him and the ocean would carry him away. Who knew what dangers lurked out there? After all, he was a civilized octopus and had no training in ocean survival. And then he saw it— the mouth of the spout from which water spewed out into the ocean. This was it—he was about to be ejected. He would never see his family again. But all at once, he was slammed against a wire-mesh screen stretched across the spout mouth.

'Ow!' Rot hissed, scrambling, grabbing hold of the screen.

He was not going to be ejected right away, it seemed. The water roared past Rot, gushing into the sea below. Rot was pinned against the screen, the surging water pounding him into the hard metal-wire-mesh. He could barely move, the wire biting into his skin.

'Uhh...this hurts!' he thought. 'Don't know how much longer I can take this!'

Suddenly, the screen swung aside and Rot shot

out of the spout like a seed being spat out.

'This is it!' he yelled, shutting his eyes.

He flew out with the water and…landed SPROING! in a net spread just below the spout.

Before he could understand what was happening, the net was yanked upwards, taking him along.

'We got him, Doc!' a voice shouted.

'Great! Bring him up here! Put him in the container!'

Bewildered, Rot felt himself being carried toward a van and then rolled into a water container. He let himself sink to the bottom, let the calm, soothing

water wash through his gills, and took a deep breath.

'Aah…' he sighed. 'That's better.'

He hurt all over, hurt like he'd never hurt before, but he had not been ejected into the sea. He'd survived.

4

'Awakooi aat lasaaoo?'

Rot stirred, sleepily. 'Mom?' he mumbled. 'I'm hungry.'

'Gaaooda. Wurriee abot yaaoula.'

Rot's eyes snapped open. He was in a water-filled tub inside a room. A female human was standing at the tub's edge, looking down at him.

'Hoaapyuu nooaatt hurrettoo?' said the human, smiling at Rot.

Rot quickly backed away to the other side of the tub.

'Don't be scared,' Reena said, soothingly. 'I'm Dr Reena Renaldo. Vet. I'll give you some food and then check if you're okay.'

Rot, of course, heard this differently and didn't

35

understand a word. Reena smiled again and poured food into the tub. Rot unwound his tentacles and reached for the food as it sank in the water. Suddenly, Reena frowned.

'That tentacle!' she exclaimed. 'It's…you're hurt!'

Rot sensed something was wrong. He stopped eating and backed away again.

'Don't worry,' Reena said, reaching into the tub. 'I'll just check that limb. Won't hurt at…urghh!!'

Brown ink splashed across Reena's face. As Reena had reached towards him, Rot's octopus defence instinct had taken over. He squirted a jet of ink at Reena, and then shooting water through his funnel, he took off, landing on the floor outside the tub.

Holding his breath, Rot ran for the open door, scuttling through it. But, of course, he forgot to not get excited, spun right around and ran back through the door into the same room. Immediately, the door slammed shut behind him. Rot turned around again and saw Reena standing with her back to the closed door.

Stepping forward, Reena said, 'Thank you for coming back. Does that mean you trust me?'

Rot slunk back. What was she saying? He didn't know—didn't want to know. All he knew was that he was trapped.

'Spun around again, eh?' a voice said in Turtle-tongue. 'Ha ha ha!'

Rot snapped around. A turtle crawled out of a tank in the corner of the room—Tumboo! Rot couldn't believe his eyes. Tumboo! His friend, Tumboo!

Reena took a cautious step forward. 'Truuss meeaaloo? Letto meeaaloo hellapoo yaouula?'

Rot scrambled back.

'Listen to me, Rot,' Tumboo said. 'This human—she's a good guy! She helped me. *And* she saved you! You can trust her.'

Rot looked at Reena, at Tumboo, and then back again at Reena. Reena opened the door behind her and stood aside. Rot looked at her, then slowly turned around, shuffled back to the tub and got into it.

'Thank you,' Reena said and shut the door again.

∽

Pictures, X-rays and video clips of Rot and his halfway

limb flashed on a screen in another room of the Sea World laboratory.

'What do you think, Dr Swami?' Reena asked a somewhat dishevelled, bespectacled gentleman sitting beside her.

This was Dr Subbu Swami or, as he put it, 'Dr Zubbu Zwami, proztheticz h'exzpert'.

'Hmm...' Dr Zwami said, 'H'I've made h'artificial limbz for dogz, catz, h'even horzez. But never for h'an h'octopuz!'

'Couldn't we try, Doctor?' Reena asked.

'H'I don't know...' Dr Zwami replied. 'Dogz, horzez, catz...they h'uze their legz bazically for movement. But h'an h'octopuz! It h'uzez h'itz tentacle for zo many thingz. H'it'z like h'a human h'arm h'and leg combined!'

'I know. And I have an answer for that!' Reena said excitedly. 'Let's make many different limbs. Then he can pick whichever one he needs at any given time!'

'What? How could *he* chooze?' Dr Zwami said. 'He'z juzt h'an h'octopuz!'

'A very special h'octopuz...er...octopus,' Reena

smiled. 'I've been testing him, Doctor. He's the cleverest creature I've ever come across!'

∽

Soothing music wafted through the lab. Rot and Tumboo sat on the edge of their tub and looked at the screen on which Reena was projecting slides.

Pointing at a sketch of Rot on the screen, Reena said, 'Ocolofashoo, thiisaaloo yaaouula.'

Rot and Tumboo looked at each other. Tumboo said, 'I think she's saying "that's you".'

'Of course that's me!' Rot said. 'He's got a halfway limb. She doesn't have to explain that!'

'She must think we're idiots!'

'I wish she'd learn to talk properly,' Rot said.

Reena repeated, 'Ocolofashoo, thiisaaloo yaaouula.'

Rot pointed at himself. Reena grinned happily, realizing she'd been understood. She clicked a remote and the slide changed. This time there were drawings of a claw, a drill, a fork, a spoon and a flashlight, all attached by holders to strange-looking pouches.

Pointing at the odd objects, Reena went, 'Thiisaaloo

acolaawo, aduriillee, ahaommeeraloo…'

'How dumb does she think we are?' Rot said. 'She's trying to tell us what those things are! We've all seen humans use them!'

'Yeah,' Tumboo agreed. 'That's a thingamajig, a watchamacallit and a…a…'

'That's a claw, a drill, a fork, a spoon and a flashlight,' Rot said.

'That's just what I was going to say!'

Rot and Tumboo did a high-one with tentacle and flipper (since they didn't have fingers, they couldn't high-five).

Reena grinned and thought, 'I'm really getting through to them!'

The next slide came up on the screen. This time it was Rot holding out his halfway limb. An arrow from the limb pointed into the holder of the flashlight.

'I've got it!' Tumboo crowed. 'You're shooting an arrow into that…that flashamajig!'

She grinned, raising her flipper for a high-one.

'I think that means my halfway limb goes into the holder of the flashlight,' Rot said.

'Really?' Tumboo asked. 'What's the arrow for? I think you're wrong, Rot.'

Reena clicked to the next slide. It was a much closer view, showing just the end of Rot's limb entering the flashlight holder.

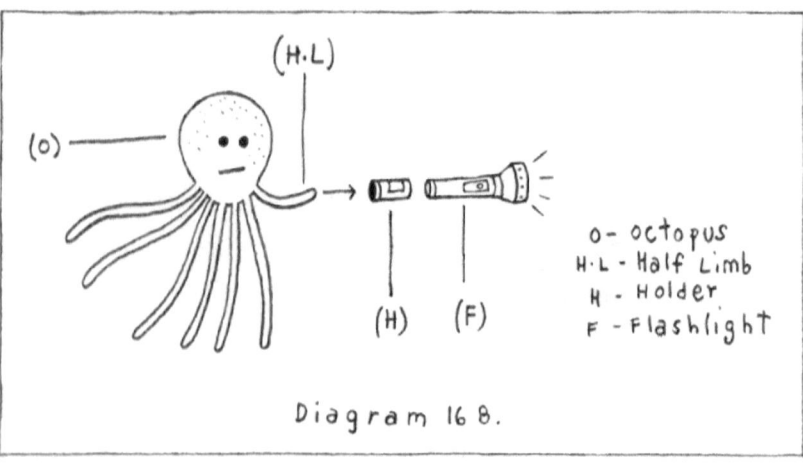

Diagram 16 8.

'What did I tell you?' Tumboo demanded. 'That's just half your halfway limb! That arrow's cut it off! See? I warned you, Rot! I knew we shouldn't have trusted her!'

'Take it easy, Tumbs. It's just a picture of the way the flashlight fits on the limb.'

'You sure?' Tumboo asked, suspiciously. 'I think we'd better...'

'Yes, yes, I'm sure,' Rot said, rolling his eyes.

The slide changed again. This one showed Rot with the flashlight attached to the end of his halfway limb, holding it straight up. A yellow, upside-down triangle perched on top of the flashlight's bulb.

'I know! I know!' Tumboo yelled. 'You're holding a bag of popcorn on that flashamacallit!'

'That's a beam of light coming out of the flashlight,' Rot sighed.

'Oh? Looks like popcorn to me and I'm never wrong about food...'

But Rot wasn't listening to her. He was looking at Reena and going 'clap-clap-clap-swish'. Reena grinned.

'I think I've done it!' she thought. 'I've managed to make him understand!' She tried to tell Rot how thrilled she was, 'Ocolofashoo, Iareaalliee haappiieethataloo unnersetaando!'

'Can you make out what she's saying, Rot?' Tumboo asked.

'Not a word,' Rot grinned. But he continued to clap anyway.

∽

The next day, Reena was helping Dr Zwami fasten the flashlight holder to Rot's halfway limb.

'A perfect fit,' Reena said, looking at the tentacle with its attached flashlight.

Rot turned the flashlight this way and that. 'Kinda cool,' he thought.

Pointing to the Start/Stop button on the flashlight, Reena said, 'Ocolofashoo, thiisaao swoiichola onu offula.'

Rot looked at the button and then at Reena, who was nodding and smiling and spouting that nonsense again. She reached forward and clicked the flashlight on. A bright beam sprang out.

'Ow!' Rot exclaimed and jumped back.

'Donaalo abe escaardoona, Ocolofashoo,' Reena

said soothingly, and slowly reached again for Rot's halfway limb. Rot cringed. Reena gently clicked the button on the flashlight and the beam disappeared. Rot blinked. So that was it. So easy. Press that button once and the light comes on. Press it again and it goes off. He straightened and held out his halfway limb. Reena looked at him expectantly. Rot pressed the button with another tentacle. The light clicked on.

'Bravo!' Reena shouted, clapping her hands. Rot switched off the light and looked at Reena.

'Baraivola!' She was gabbling nonsense again, but she was looking pleased. Rot switched on the light and pointed it at Reena. She half-covered her eyes, laughing.

'He's got it,' Tumboo said. 'I think he's got it!'

Rot focussed the beam on Tumboo.

'He's got it! By George, he's got it!' Tumboo shouted, striking a theatrical pose.

Unfortunately, posing like that meant that Tumboo's flippers had to let go of the tub-edge. She promptly fell back into the tub with an enormous splash!

The afternoon wore on with Dr Zwami and Reena working on the tools. They were astonishing gadgets, capable of being folded down to the size of a toothbrush and then snapping open fully when required. One by one, a claw, a fork, a screwdriver, a hammer, a spoon, even a needle, was attached to Rot's limb. Amazingly, Rot learnt to use them in no time at all (even managing to thread the needle)! Finally, they tried on the drill.

'It'z battery-powered,' Dr Zwami said to Rot as he attached the drill to Rot's halfway limb.

Of course, what Rot heard was, 'Itooso bateefas pavulltoo.'

But he knew what he was supposed to do. Even a baby octopus could tell that the green switch was for 'start' and the red one for 'stop'. Rot placed the bit of the drill against a wooden board that Reena held. Then he curled another tentacle towards the drill and pressed the green switch. A loud, whining noise filled the lab as the drill started vibrating. Reena looked at the bit of the drill, expecting it to spin and bore a hole in the wood. But it remained completely still. However, something else did start spinning—the handle of the drill. And since Rot was attached to the handle, so did he! He spun up and down and round and round like a leaf stuck on a car wheel.

'StopitsomeoneIwanttogetoffstopppiiiiittt!' Rot yelled, his tentacles going 'flapatooey, flipatooey, flapatooey' as he revolved.

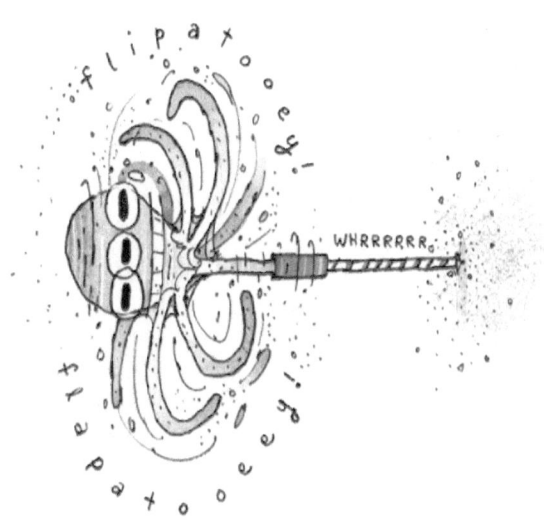

Faintly, he heard Reena shouting, 'Stopaloo! Docuturudo sumaathinggaoo!'

Rot wished she'd stop yammering and do something. His insides were feeling more and more like a well-stirred milkshake. Finally, Reena managed to hit the red switch and Rot tumbled to a halt. Tumboo clapped enthusiastically.

'That was terrific!' she hooted. 'Again?'

5

eanwhile, back at the Octopus Den, everyone was wondering where Rot had gone. His parents were troubled, searching every part of Sea World. The only place they didn't look was the Killer Whale and Shark Lair. No right-minded water creature would go there.

As Rot's classmate Irrit8 said, 'Well, if Rot's got in there, he isn't coming back!'

Po8 promptly came up with a limerick he thought hilarious:

When the shark made a meal of Rot8,
He commented on what he just ate,
'I won't complain about it
But there was a missing bit,
I wish next time they'd serve a full plate!'

'That's cruel!' said Kissmek8.

'And in bad taste!' said First8.

'Yeah, that's what the shark thought, too!' Irrit8 cracked.

'Ha ha ha!' his gang roared. 'B…bad taste! Ha ha ha ha!'

But Rot's Mom, Delic, ignored all this. She knew that Rot was too clever to wander into the Whale and Shark Lair. And when she learnt from Tumboo's mother, Mrs Turn Turtle, that Tumboo was missing too, she knew that the children had gone off somewhere together.

'But I really worried!' Delic said (in Fishy, which no one spoke well). 'Not like Rot do something like this!'

'Tumboo don't miss single meal,' Mrs Turn Turtle wailed. 'And now she missed seven!'

Tumboo, of course, wasn't missing any meals.

'Now I know what a whale feels like!' she gurgled as she chomped and chewed her way through the unending supply of food brought by Reena's assistants. This was heaven! All she had to do was eat while Rot did the work!

'H'EEN-credi-bull!' Dr Zwami said. 'He'z learnt

to h'uze h'every tool h'I've tried him with!'

'I know,' Reena replied. 'His IQ is at the human "very high" level. But there's something more. Take a look at this, Dr Zwami...'

She played a video clip of the moments when Rot had awoken after his rescue. They watched Reena trying to soothe him, talk to him and then touch his halfway limb. Acting on instinct, Rot had squirted her with ink and then, shooting water through his funnel, had rocketed out of the tub, flown over Reena and landed on the floor behind her.

'H'I didn't know h'octopuzez could do that!' Dr Zwami exclaimed.

'All of them have this funnel through which they can shoot water and travel really fast in emergencies. They've been known to reach speeds of 40 kilometres per hour in water!'

'H'EEN-credi-bull!'

'Yes,' Reena agreed. 'But this one is something special. I calculated the force at which he'd shot water through his funnel to take off like that. If he were travelling through water, he'd probably reach a speed of 70 kilometres per hour!'

'H'underwater? H'EEM-pozzi-bull!'

'But true,' Reena said. 'I think his lack of a limb has led to over-development in other areas. With his intelligence, his speed and the tools we've made for him, he's unlike any other octopus in the world!'

6

Everyone in Goa knows June is the month when the monsoon rolls in. Sometimes the rains start in a gentle, friendly way with light showers checking in, just to let everyone know that it's time to get out the umbrellas and raincoats. And sometimes the monsoon just explodes with crashing thunder and lightning and the wind and rain barrel in. This year was one of the unfriendly ones. The sky opened and rain bucketed down with no intention of

stopping. Ponds and lakes filled up and poured their water into rivers that rushed through the countryside like roaring trains, foaming and frothing to the sea.

To the water creatures, though, the boiling rain on the pool-surface made little difference. They went about their business in the calm depths of the water, unconcerned with what was happening above—particularly the octopuses and turtles who had more important things to think of. By now Clarin and Delic and Mr and Mrs Turn Turtle were frantic with worry. Rot and Tumboo had still not returned and it was obvious something had happened to them. Organizing themselves into search parties, the octopuses and turtles fanned out, heading for the nooks and crannies of the various pools of Sea World.

'And stay together,' Clarin said (in Fishy) to the youngsters in the teams. 'Last thing we need anyone else going missing.'

∽

At the lab building, Dr Zwami scurried in to get out of the rain.

'H'een-credi-bull!' he said, as he shut his umbrella.

'H'it'z really coming down h'outzide!'

'Did you get it?' Reena asked, hurrying up to him.

Dr Zwami grinned, unwrapping something from a waterproof cover.

'Here h'it h'iz,' he said. 'The H'OMPB!'

Proudly, he held it up. It was a flat belt of flexible fibre, which had various pouches for Rot's tools.

'The "HOMPB"?' Reena asked, taking the belt from Dr Zwami.

'The "H'Octopuz Multi-Purpoze Belt"!' Dr Zwami replied. 'But that'z a mouthful. So h'I juzt call h'it the H'OMPB! What do you think?'

'Oh, I'm sure we can come up with something better,' Reena said.

Dr Zwami looked crestfallen, but Reena didn't notice.

'H'anyway,' Dr Zwami said, 'let me show you how h'it workz.' He picked up the screwdriver, folded it over and pushed it into its pouch in the belt.

'Now he juzt h'inzertz hiz halfway limb h'into the pouch,' said Dr Zwami, demonstrating the action with an imitation limb. The holder at the mouth of the

pouch automatically locked on to the 'limb'. Dr Zwami withdrew it and snapped it forward like a whip. The screwdriver popped open. Reena laughed, delighted.

'Good, h'eh?' Dr Zwami asked.

'EEN-credi-bull!' Reena said, smiling.

Outside, the Sea World pools were humming with activity as octopus and turtle search parties looked everywhere (except in the Killer Whale and Shark Lair). They'd asked the dolphins and seals, walruses and platypuses and just about everyone, but nobody had news of the missing pair.

'Look,' Clarin said, as the teams gathered together.

'I know you other things to do. If anyone need go home, you can.'

'Of course not!' said almost all the octopuses and turtles. 'We not going quit until find them!'

'Thank you,' Clarin said. 'Try this way. Turtles—you look where octopuses already search. Octopuses—we go where turtles been. This way we double-check. Should find them!'

'Sound good,' almost everyone said. 'Let's go!'

They scattered in different directions. Not everyone, though—*almost* everyone.

'Feel like spending the afternoon searching for those two?' drawled Irrit8.

'No way!' Po8 said.

'School's closed, you know,' Irrit said. 'Let's go see if we can do something to upset the teachers!'

Laughing, they swam off by themselves.

In the Sea World lab, Reena had just finished showing Rot how to use the H'OMPB (she still hadn't found a better name for it).

'Did you understand?' Reena asked Rot.

He didn't understand her words, but her meaning was clear. It was so very easy—all Rot had to do was insert his halfway limb into any of the belt's pouches. And when he withdrew his limb, the tool in the pouch would come out with it—as part of the limb. Now he could do more things with his one halfway tentacle than any other octopus could do with eight whole ones!

However, there was just one hitch—where to fasten the belt on Rot. Reena had decided that the only place for the belt was around Rot's head. It would also be a fashion statement—he would be the only octopus with a bandana!

'Now hold still,' Reena said to Rot as she wound the belt around his head. 'There you go! You look like a bloodthirsty pirate!' she laughed.

She held up a mirror for Rot, but the moment Rot moved, the belt slipped down his head, completely covering his eyes and mouth.

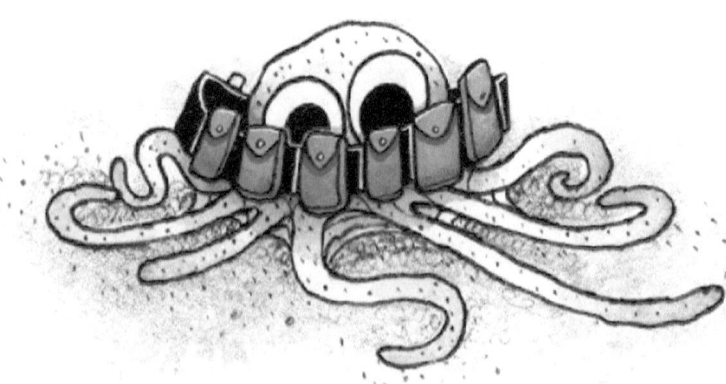

'Hey! That really improves your looks!' Tumboo cackled.

'I think we'll just tighten it a bit,' Reena said.

She positioned the belt around Rot's head again. But it was like tightening a rubber band around jelly. When making the belt, Dr Zwami had forgotten that octopuses have no bony skeleton. The more Reena tightened the belt, the narrower Rot's head became.

And when Rot climbed back into the tub and took a deep breath, his head's shape snapped back to normal and the belt shot right off the top!

'Ha ha ha!' Tumboo roared.

Rot grinned.

'This isn't working,' Reena said.

'No, h'it h'izn't,' Dr Zwami agreed. 'Let me work h'on that belt.'

He took the tools out of the holders and carried the belt back into the workroom of the lab.

'Soarriio,' Reena said to Rot. 'Bee baakalo summtaiimu.'

She followed Dr Zwami out. Rot and Tumboo looked at the tools scattered around.

'You'll never be able to carry all that stuff,' Tumboo said.

'If only I had a shell like yours,' Rot sighed. 'I could put in all that and more…'

Suddenly, Rot and Tumboo looked at each other.

'Hey!' Rot said.

'I could carry the stuff for you!' Tumboo said.

'We could be partners!' Rot said, excitedly.

'Like…like…' said Tumboo.

'Like Tintin and Captain Had…no, Ms Haddock!' said Rot, who never missed a cartoon movie shown at Sea World.

'Like…' Tumboo said.

'Like Asterix and Ms Obelix!' said Rot.

'Like Curry and Ms Rice!' Tumboo shouted, finally finding the perfect comparison.

They high-one'd each other.

7

Outside, the rain poured as if it would never stop.

'Some of the pools are getting full,' the Sea World Senior Supervisor said, worriedly. 'We'd better drain some water out.'

'Yef, fir,' said the Junior Super (he had a noticeable lisp).

'Pools D, G, M and S,' the Senior Super said. 'Lower the levels by seven feet.'

'Fertainly, fir. Right away, fir.'

Huddling under an umbrella, the Junior Super splashed through the rain, looking for the pool attendants. A storm warning had been flashed and most attendants had left early. Luckily, there seemed to be one attendant who hadn't left as yet. He was getting soaked in the rain, struggling to straighten a signboard he'd knocked over.

'Hey!' the Junior Super called. 'Come with me. We've got to leffen the water in the poolf.'

'Poolf?' the attendant asked, puzzled.

'The poolf!' the Junior Super shouted, pointing at the pools. 'Can't you fee the poolf?!'

'Oh,' the attendant said, getting it. 'Yes, boss.'

'We've got to lower the water by feven feet,' the Junior Super cried, trying to make himself heard above the howling wind. 'I'll take Poolf D and G. You take M and F.'

'Yes, boss,' the attendant said.

'Go, man! Don't juft ftand there!' the Junior Super shouted. 'And liffen! What'f your name?'

'Claude, boss. Claude Custado.'

What happened after this wasn't entirely Clumsy Claude's fault. He had heard 'M' and 'F' so he hurried over to Pool M. The Junior Super was right—it was nearly full, about to overflow. This time, though, Clumsy remembered that he had to clear the pool of water creatures before opening the drains. Quickly, he opened up the valves at the edges of the pool.

The water was funnelled toward the valves and every water creature in Pool M was swept into neighbouring pools. Next, Clumsy opened the drains and lowered the level of the water by exactly 'feven' feet. Then he rushed off to the other pool on his list: 'F'. Reaching the pool, he noticed that it wasn't at overflow level— nowhere near it.

'Dis funny,' he mused. 'Why dey want to lower de water level of dis pool? Dis just half full!' He stood for a moment, scratching his head. But rain was pelting down, Clumsy Claude was cold and he wanted to get home.

'Fergeddit, I's not arguing with de "boff",' he muttered.

If Clumsy had just thought about it, he'd have realized that when his 'boff' said 'F', he meant 'S'. But he was not clever enough for that. He opened the valves and funnelled the water creatures out of Pool F. Then he drained seven feet of water out of the pool, finished up and went home.

Meanwhile, over in Pool S, water continued to rise, nearing overflow level.

∽

'This not working,' Clarin said (in Fishy) to Mrs Turn Turtle.

'Yes,' she agreed. 'Humans moving water creatures from one pool to other. Searching parties losting.'

From which exchange Clarin understood that the search parties were getting lost.

'All right,' he said. 'We take break. Everyone go home one hour. Start again when humans stop water movement. All agree?'

Everyone agreed and drifted home. *Almost* everyone. The two that didn't agree were far away in Pool R—the reef pool. For that's where the water creature school was.

'Okay,' Irrit8 chuckled, as he surveyed the mess they had made of the school. 'We've squirted ink everywhere, we've upturned the desks, downturned the chairs, and left turtle and seven-limbed octopus tracks everywhere. Rot and that turtle soup bowl are going to be in b-i-i-i-i-g trouble! Let's go.'

'Wait,' Po8 said. 'We've got to leave a message for the teachers to find!'

He picked up eight pieces of chalk and started scrawling on the blackboard, writing eight lines at once. (Octopuses have been known to do this. Which is why their teachers never try to punish them by giving them lines.)

'What are you doing?' Irrit demanded. 'If you write poetry, everyone will know it was you!'

'Not this time,' Po said, cackling wickedly.

✏

In the lab, a dejected Reena and a forlorn Dr Zwami made their way back to Rot and Tumboo.

'I'm sorry,' Reena said to Rot. 'We've not been able to solve the belt problem. We'll need more time.'

'Let'z put h'away the tools and try h'again tomorrow,' Dr Zwami said. He looked around. All his precious miniature tools had vanished! 'B...but the toolz!' he exclaimed. 'Where h'are they?'

'No one came here,' Reena said, equally puzzled. 'Where could they be?' She looked at Rot. 'Do you think he...?'

Rot and Tumboo saw Reena and Dr Zwami look at them and blather nonsensically, as usual.

'Time to give them a surprise,' Rot said. 'Tumboo, the flashlight, please.'

Tumboo reached into her shell and pulled out a pouch.

'Look at that!' Reena exclaimed. 'They've put the tools into the turtle's shell! They've solved the problem!'

'H'een-credi-bull!'

Ignoring the human gibberish, Rot fastened the pouch on to his halfway limb and then snapped it forward. Out popped a...spoon!

'Oops!' Tumboo said.

'Oh, that's wonderful!' Reena gushed, clapping.

'H'een-credi-bull!'

Rot turned to Tumboo. 'Do you think you could give me the flashlight *this* time?' he asked, sarcastically.

'Yup, s...sure,' Tumboo said. 'I don't know how that happened.'

She pulled out another pouch and handed it over. Rot attached it to his limb and whipped it forward. Out sprang a...screwdriver!

Reena clapped with admiration. 'Isn't that marvellous? The octopus asks for a tool and the turtle gives him exactly what he asks for!'

Rot didn't say anything—just glared at Tumboo.

'O…one flashlight coming up,' Tumboo said, nervously.

She handed Rot another pouch. Rot fastened it on and snapped it forward. A fork appeared with its prongs holding a slice of pizza.

Reena giggled.

'Oh, oh! That's left over from breakfast,' Tumboo said.

Rot said nothing—just looked at her.

'What?' Tumboo said, defensively. 'You know turtles love pizza!'

'That's terrific!' Reena said. 'They're finding new uses for it, themselves! I think they're ready to go back in the pool. Don't you agree, Dr Zwami?'

Dr Zwami just goggled, too astonished even to say 'H'een-credi-bull'!

8

An hour had passed, and in the main pool, the search parties had gathered again.

'All right,' Clarin said (in Fishy). 'Humans no move water creatures no more. Time we began. Turtles, you east and north. We, west and south.'

'We look everywhere again,' Delic said. 'Sure to find them.'

'Who are we looking for?' a voice piped up in Turtle-tongue.

'Don't be silly, Tumboo!' Mr Turn Turtle said. 'You know we're looking for Rot and...*Tumboo!* Is that you??'

'All forty kilos of me!' Tumboo said, grinning.

'Tumboo! Tumboo! Where have you been?!' Mrs Turn Turtle scolded and laughed (at the same time).

'Where Rot?' Delic demanded. 'With you?'

'I'm right here, Mom!'

'Rot! We were so worried! What happened to you?'

'Oh, nothing,' Rot said, casually. 'Just sucked into the drain and almost ejected into the sea.'

'What?!'

'The drain??'

'Ejected into the sea?!'

There was such a hubbub and clamour that for a few minutes no one noticed the emergency siren. But octopuses and turtles have very sharp hearing and they gradually became aware of the *'wheet-wheet-wheet'* sound slicing through the pool. And then they saw other water creatures hurrying, scurrying, rushing, panicking.

'What happen?' Clarin asked a passing seal. 'Why emergency alarm?'

'Pool S!' the seal shouted. 'It overflow!'

'So it overflow,' Tumboo said. 'Big deal!'

'You don't know who live in Pool S?' a dolphin yelled as it rushed by. 'Sharks!'

'And killer whales!'

❧

'How could this happen?' the Senior Supervisor yelled as he puffed through the downpour towards Pool S. 'I had ordered you to open the drains and lower the water levels!'

'Yef, fir,' the Junior Super babbled, running alongside his 'boff'. 'We did it, fir! I don't know what went wrong, fir!'

'I'll do it myself!' the Senior Super said, angrily. 'If they get out, who knows what those killer whales and sharks could do!'

There was no need for panic, though. As soon as they realized what was happening, the water creatures had decided not to go anywhere near Pool S. Each species took a quick headcount to make sure everyone had gotten away safely.

'All here,' said the walruses.

'We okay,' said the turtles.

'We one too many!' said the penguins, but they were never very good at counting.

There was just one species that came up short.

'Where's Irrit8?' an octopus asked.

'Have you seen Po8 anywhere?' another octopus inquired. 'Has anyone seen them?'

But no one had.

Meanwhile at the school, Po8 said, 'I think it's my masterpiece!' as he admired the poem he had scrawled on the blackboard:

Ink we squirt and chalk we smear,
All tables do we turn,
Not underwater if we were
All lessons we would burn!

We smash and vandalize the school
And leave nary a clue,
If we weren't in a silly pool,
Just think what we could do!

By teachers are we always sought,
But water wipes out tracks,
So just to see if we get caught,
We'll help you with some facts.

We're no strangers to you, pal,

Jyotin Goel

You know us as two chums,
We are but a guy and gal,
Two no-good, lazy bums!

Since I'm the gal, I'll go first,
'Bout me I'll let you know,
I'm so very fat that I could burst
But still eat more and more!

Turtle am I of green pigment,
My size: X X X Large,
Though I've been called 'blimp' and 'tent',
It hurts when I'm called 'barge'!

Now I'm the guy, all orange-pink,
I hope to be a hero,
One of these days I won't (I think)
Go in circles like a zero!

Opus am I but not an Oct,
No, not an octopus,
For one limb less I've oft been mocked,
'He's just a Septopus!'

Now you may think we make this mess
'Cos we're angry and/or bitter,
But again you need to guess
Why we smash, spoil, litter!

It's so much fun to trash one's school,
It's just this one big lark,
It's so easy, it's so cool,
It's just a swim in the park!

No more lessons, no more sums,
And if you're grateful to us,
Then three cheers for two lazy bums,
The Turtle and Septopus!

'Ha ha ha!' Irrit8 roared. 'That's terrific!'

Po8 grinned. 'Is that a good enough clue to who messed up the school?'

'It's a signed confession!' Irrit said, slapping Po on his back. 'Rot and Tumboo—they're grounded!'

Outside, the Senior Super stood at the edge of Pool S, looking at the water level. It was a few inches below the top—dropping, but slowly, too slowly.

'It's the rain!' he groaned. 'It's coming down harder than ever. We barely get water out and it fills up again.'

And then he saw it—a shark fin on the surface of the pool! In a moment, another one broke the surface, and then another. They tore circles in the pool, slicing through the water. Lightning crashed all around. The Senior Super stepped back. This was getting dangerous. He needed to call the keepers to calm the agitated creatures. Suddenly, he froze. A HUGE fin emerged from the water followed by the gigantic black-and-white head of a killer whale. The jaws opened for a moment revealing row upon row of knife-like teeth. Then they snapped shut and the enormous body turned over and vanished in the depths below. The Senior Super stood as if turned to stone.

'Did you fee that, fir?' exclaimed a voice behind the Senior Super.

He glanced around. The Junior Super stood there, goggling at the water.

'That was Rakfuf!' the Junior Super cried.

'Rakfuf?'

'The whale, fir! He'f a mean one. The keeperf fay he'f the hardeft to control. A bad-tempered brute, fir!'

The Senior Super turned back to look at the sharks churning through the water. This was no act for tourists. There were no keepers throwing fish to the giant creatures as a reward for feats well performed. The pool was overflowing, the creatures were disturbed by the fury of the storm. This was a disaster in the making.

And then it happened. The killer whale shot up from the depths and leapt into the air. For a moment it was outlined against the sky as lightning blazed around it.

Then the whale curved its body in a mighty arc

POOL-R

and hurtled across the pool edge into the neighbouring pool—Pool R, the reef pool! It crashed into the water and plunged, disappearing in a moment.

'What was that?' gasped Irrit8, as he picked himself up.

There had been an enormous splash and then fierce currents of water had swept through the reef, knocking them over.

'It was a meteor!' Po8 croaked. 'This is what happened to the dinosaurs! We're going to be extincted!'

'Extincted?'

'A new word I came up with. We poets do it all the time.'

A huge, dark shadow passed directly over them.

'That's no meteor!' Irrit squeaked.

Cautiously, they crept to a hole in the reef and peered out. Nothing. They shuffled silently to another hole, carefully looking out again. A gigantic shape barrelled past right in front of their eyes, water rippling in its wake. Irrit and Po scrambled back, terrified.

'A m...monster!' Po stuttered. 'An alien m... monster from the m...m...meteor!'

'That...that's no monster!' Irrit quaked. 'That's a k...killer w...whale!'

9

The '*wheet-wheet-wheet*' of the alarm sounded all around Sea World. Frantically, the Senior and Junior Supers ordered the keepers and workers about. Reena, responding to the alarm, hurried to the Senior Super.

'The alarm—what's happened?' she asked.

'Rakfuf!' the Senior Super answered.

Reena didn't understand.

'Rakfuf?'

'Rakfuf! Rakfuf!' repeated the Senior Super. 'The killer whale!'

'Oh, Rakshus!' Reena said.

'Rakshus?'

'Yes, Rakshus, the demon,' Reena said. 'The killer whale. What about him?'

'*Rakshus…*' the Senior Super embarrassedly muttered, shooting a glare at the Junior Super, 'he's gotten into the reef pool!'

'What?! Are there any other species there?' Reena demanded.

'We don't know,' the Junior Super said. 'But we've ftopped the valvef. No water creature can now get into the reef pool acfidentally.'

'But if there's any creature already there,' Reena said, 'the whale will just…'

∞

'Whale…tail…jail…fail…' Po8 muttered, terrified.

'W…what are you doing?' Irrit8 whispered.

'C…can't help it…bit…sit… When I'm scared, I rhyme…time…mime…dime… It's poetic reaction… faction…action…'

'Well, shut up!' Irrit hissed. 'That creature outside doesn't know we're here yet. But if you keep up that racket, we're goners!'

'…honours…corners…yawners…'

Irrit clapped a tentacle on Po's mouth, cutting off his runaway rhymes.

'Listen,' Irrit whispered, 'the school goes right to the top of the reef, above the surface—where the seals and penguins have their classes. There's a way up there from within. Let's go!'

Po looked at Irrit, horrified. He couldn't say anything but he shook his head violently, making very clear his opinion of Irrit's plan.

'Look, Po,' Irrit said, 'it's safer up there! We'll be at least six feet above the surface—the whale won't be able to get us. Down here we're sitting ducks! Once the whale finds out we're here, he'll just bust into the reef!'

Irrit headed for the passage to the top, dragging Po along.

'Look!' Reena shouted from above, pointing to the reef. 'There are others still there!'

Irrit8 and Po8 emerged from one of the topmost crevices of the reef and slithered on to the flat area where the seals and penguins normally gathered.

'We're safe,' Irrit said, carefully looking around. 'That monster doesn't know we're up here!'

He removed his tentacle from Po's mouth. Po tried to take a deep breath, but they were out of the water.

'There's just one problem with your brilliant plan… man…tan…' wheezed Po. 'We need to get back into the water as quickly as we can…ran…pan…'

'We'll slip down below the surface every few minutes and stock up on our breathing,' Irrit said. 'Then we'll sneak back here. I'm sure in a little while the whale will get bored and go away.'

But Rakshus wasn't going anywhere. He was angry. Staying just below the surface, he powered around Pool R, his fin carving through the water like a huge axe. The water level in this pool was low so he couldn't leap into the next pool without crashing into the surrounding walls. He was trapped. And hungry. Round and round he went but there were no other fish there—nothing at all to eat. Just then, he noticed the humans at the pool-edge point to the top of the reef. Was something there, after all? Rakshus decided to check it out himself. He backed up, then charged at the reef and leapt into the air. He soared over the reef—and saw them! Two octopuses!

Rakshus hit the water on the other side of the reef and sank underwater.

'D...did he see us...bus...fuss...?' Po croaked through his chattering beak.

'I d...don't know...' Irrit whispered. 'I th...think...'

But we'll never know what he thought for the next moment his words froze in his mouth. Rakshus' fin had broken the surface of the water and was heading straight for the reef.

'He saw us!' Irrit breathed, horrified.

'...muss...plus...truss...'

With the force of a runaway train, Rakshus slammed into the reef. It shuddered as large chunks broke away. Po almost fell over the edge but Irrit grabbed him and pulled him back.

'Don't let me fall...call...wall...tall...!'

Rakshus turned around and swam away.

'He's trying to knock them down into the water!' Reena cried.

'Can't we do something?' the Senior Super pleaded.

'We'll have to knock the whale out! I'll get the tranquilizer gun. It's the only hope for those octopuses!'

'Look, a turtle!' the Junior Super shouted. 'And another octopuf!'

'What?' Reena cried, spinning around. 'Where?'

Barely visible through the lashing rain, Rot and Tumboo scuttled over the walkways between the pools. With his sharp octopus vision, Rot could clearly see the terrifying scene in Pool R. He saw Irrit and Po cower on the top of the reef and the whale fin race towards them. He heard the thump as Rakshus rammed the reef and saw the octopuses desperately try to hang on.

'C'mon, Tumboo!' Rot shouted, as his friend lagged behind.

'Coming, coming,' Tumboo puffed, moving as fast over ground as an overweight turtle could.

'Oh, no!' Reena cried. 'Stop them!'

She ran forward followed by the Junior Super and some keepers but Rot and Tumboo had already reached the edge of Pool R.

'Oh, shellfish!' Tumboo exclaimed, looking at the gigantic killer whale churning through the water below. 'Do we really want to do this, Rot? I mean, how's the world a better place if we save Irrit and Po?'

'No time for that now!' Rot replied. 'Here comes the lab lady!' Looking down at the pool he shouted,

'Bombs awayyyyyyy!' and leapt in.

'Look out belowwww!' Tumboo yelled as she tilted her forty kilos over the edge. She hit the pool with a huge splash and sank like a fat boulder.

'That was my octopus! My turtle!' Reena cried. 'We've got to save them!'

∽

Rot and Tumboo let themselves sink to the bottom of the pool.

'What do we do now?' Tumboo asked.

'Shh!' Rot hissed as an enormous form loomed over them. But the whale was focused on just two things—the reef and the octopuses on top. He charged though the water again and crashed against the cement of the artificial reef. The entire structure shook dangerously. Rot and Tumboo heard a faint voice from top go 'Ow!' followed by another voice, '...cow...now...chow...'

'We've got to get Irrit and Po out of this pool,' Rot whispered. 'Give me the flashlight.'

Tumboo pulled out a pouch from her shell.

'You sure this is it?' Rot asked, looking at it doubtfully.

'Yup,' Tumboo answered. 'See? I wrote an "F" on it. For "Flashlight"!'

'Okay. I've got a plan. Wait here and do nothing, Tumbs. I'm going into that reef.'

'Going into the reef? You call that a plan?' Tumboo demanded, but Rot was already swimming away fast. Tumboo muttered, 'The only bit I liked was "wait here and do nothing"!'

10

On top of the reef, Irrit8 and Po8 were gasping. They needed oxygen in their lungs and the only way to get that was to let water pass through their gills.

'We'll have to go down, Po,' Irrit wheezed. 'We're out of oxygen.'

'We're doomed,' Po gasped. 'If that monster hits the reef while we're down there, we're dead...red... fed...'

'We've got no choice, Po. Come on.'

They scrambled into the reef and slipped underwater.

'Aah...' Irrit breathed. 'That's better.'

'W...where's that creature...teacher...preacher...?'

'Boo!'

'Ow!' Irrit screeched, stumbling back and slamming into the reef wall.

'Wh…who's that?' Po gasped.

'Just li'l ol' me!' Rot said, floating forward.

'Don't scare us like that!' Irrit complained. 'And where did you come from, anyway? What're you doing here?'

'Well, I've been admiring a poem on the blackboard,' Rot grinned. 'I especially like the "Septopus" bit.'

'Oh!' Po tried to laugh it off. 'Heh-heh. Just a joke! Y…you see, octopuses have eight limbs but you've got just seven, so "*Sept*-opus"… heh-heh…not very f…funny…honey…bunny…'

He trailed off as Rot looked at him stonily.

'All right, now listen to me,' Rot said. 'We've got to get out of here before that whale hits this reef again.'

'Yeah, let's go!' Irrit said, heading for the pathway to the top of the reef.

Rot stopped him. 'Not that way! He'll smash the reef and get you in the end. We've got to get to the ladder on the far wall and climb out of the pool.'

'Excuse me!' Irrit hissed. 'There's a five-ton whale out there that might object to that!'

'I'll go first,' Rot whispered. 'Get him to go after me. When he's distracted, go for the ladder quick as you can!'

'You're mad!' Irrit gasped. 'He'll tear you to bits!'

Rot grinned. 'He'll have to catch me first!'

Rakshus turned around at the far end of the pool and glared beady-eyed at the reef. This time he'd knock it over for sure. With a heave of his huge tail, he shot forward. Suddenly, he saw an octopus emerge from the reef—not above the surface where he had last seen them but underwater, right where Rakshus was headed. It appeared the octopus had given up. Good! Rakshus' nose was feeling a little tender from its repeated hammering against the reef and he didn't want to slam into it again if he could help it.

Rot saw Rakshus coming straight at him like a monster from a nightmare.

'What am I doing?' he thought. His voice was a little shaky as he shouted to Irrit and Po, 'Remember! As soon as he chases me, go fast for the ladder!'

'This is crazy...hazy...lazy...' said Po.

'Shut up!' snapped Irrit8, really irritated!

Rot stood still in the water watching Rakshus

loom nearer and nearer. With just a few feet to go, Rakshus opened his mouth wide. The rows of jagged teeth gleamed. They closed in on Rot and the great jaws snapped shut. But all that Rakshus had bitten into was water—Rot was no longer there! The moment the jaws had started to close, Rot shot water through his funnel and rocketed away through the pool at unbelievable speed.

'Hooo, wow!' Irrit whistled, peering out from the reef through a peephole. 'Look at Rot go, go, GO, Po!'

'Hey! Rhyming's *my* thing!'

Rakshus turned around, confused. He couldn't believe it. One moment his jaws were about to grab their prey and the next moment there was nothing. He saw Rot speed away and he narrowed his eyes. So! The octopus wanted to play? Rakshus was game for that! He snorted with anger and tore after Rot.

'That's our cue, Po!' Irrit cried. 'C'mon!'

'Out there? With the wh…wh…wh…?' For the first time ever, words failed Po.

'Let's go, Po!' Irrit urged, grabbing Po's tentacle and trying to drag him along.

Po shuddered with fear. All at once, his eyes closed,

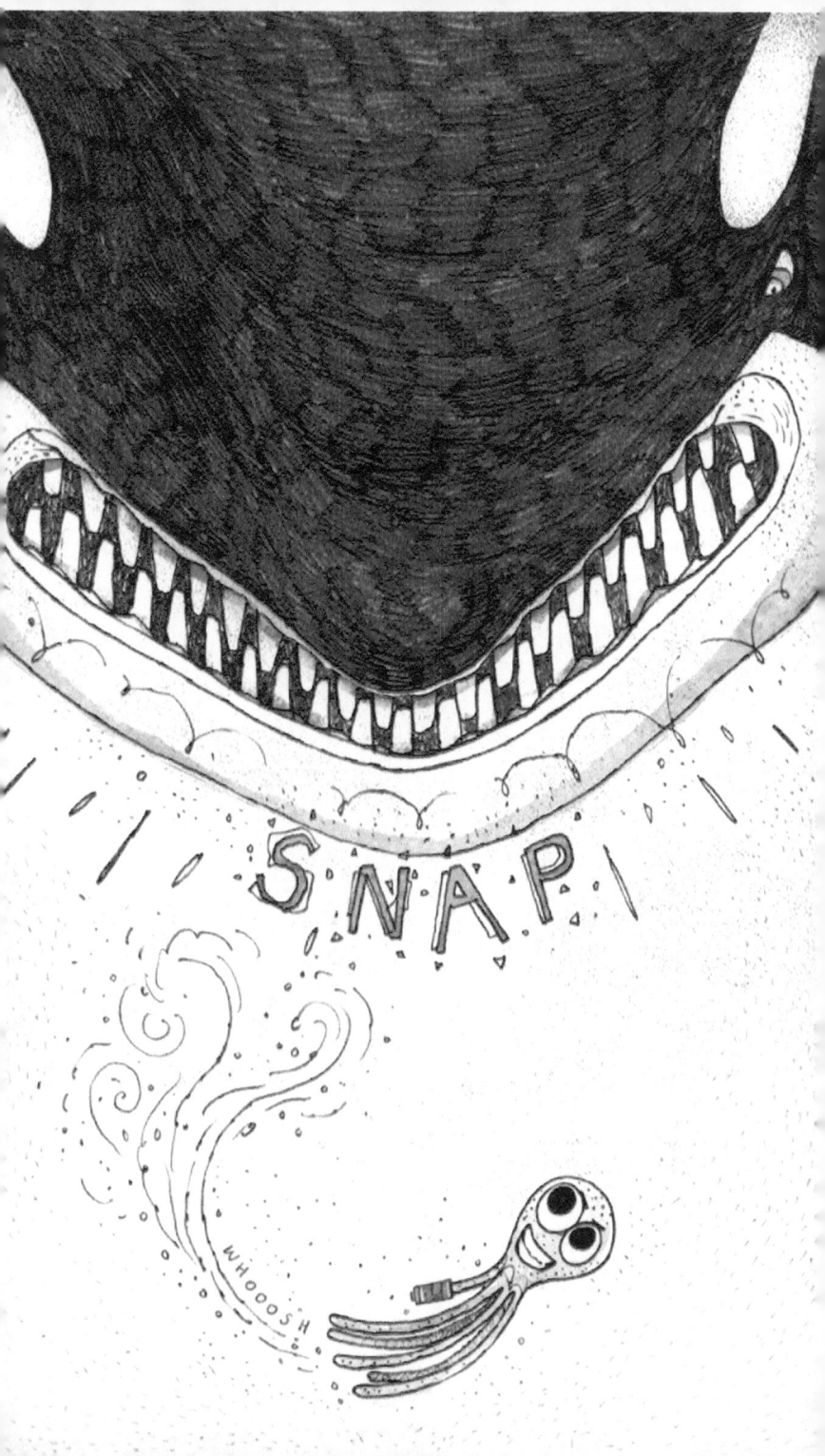

he went limp and collapsed in Irrit's tentacles.

'Oh, great!' Irrit said. 'He's fainted.'

At the other end of the pool, Rot was playing a deadly game of tag with Rakshus. He allowed the whale to get as close as possible and at the very last minute, shot away. Seeing that Irrit and Po had still not emerged from the reef, Rot headed for the opposite corner. Unluckily, this was exactly the place where Tumboo had hidden herself.

'Hey!' Tumboo hissed to Rot. 'Don't bring him here!'

The protest was too late. Rakshus was hot on Rot's trail, with his gaping mouth and those awful teeth.

'Eek!' squeaked Tumboo and dived into her shell just as Rakshus grabbed her in his terrible jaws. The teeth bit down hard on Tumboo.

'Ow!' Rakshus roared as he felt his teeth almost snap on the rock-hard shell. He spat out the offending morsel.

'Pthooh! Taste terrible!' he growled as he turned, chasing after the more chewy octopus.

Tumboo popped her head out of her shell. 'I've

never been so insulted!' she said, grinning.

But for Rot this was no laughing matter. He was getting tired. He knew that he could not keep up this speed for very long but the whale, with its untold strength, could go on and on. Sooner or later, Rot knew, he'd be caught. Where were Irrit and Po? By now they should have been halfway up the ladder, getting out of the pool. And then he saw them. They were sputtering along, still yards away from the ladder. They were going so slowly—was Irrit carrying Po? Rot had to do something right away. Trying to get the whale as far as possible from Irrit and Po, Rot streaked away in the opposite direction. Rakshus followed him like a monstrous eagle after its prey.

'Oh, no!' Tumboo groaned. 'Here they come again!' She quickly popped back into her shell.

Glancing over his shoulder, Rot saw that Irrit and Po had made it to the ladder. Now if only the whale could remain distracted another few seconds while they climbed…

'The flashlight!' Rot thought. 'I'd forgotten that! That'll get this pea-brained monster's attention!'

He whipped forward the pouch fastened to his

halfway limb and out sprang a...box with a red button!

'What the heck is this?' Rot thought, baffled.

But at that moment, across the pool at the ladder, Po suddenly opened his eyes as if jerking awake from a nightmare and yelled, 'Aah! Don't let him get me!'

'Shhh!' Irrit shushed, clapping his tentacle on to Po's motor-mouth. Uselessly.

Rakshus glanced around and saw the octopuses on the ladder. This was easier prey! He swung around and steamed towards Irrit and Po.

Rot shouted, 'Tumboo!' rapping on her shell.

Out popped Tumboo.

'Where's my flashlight?' Rot demanded, shoving the box under Tumboo's nose. 'How is this an "F"?'

'Oops!' Tumboo said. 'Is that a fire alarm? I'd forgotten...I had two "Fs"...or was it three? I think I have a fone in here, too.'

'A phone begins with a "P"!' Rot snapped. 'What am I doing? I have no time for this!'

He raced after the whale, hoping to get ahead of him before he reached Irrit and Po. But he knew he wouldn't get there in time. Po and Irrit stood frozen with fear staring at the whale that was almost upon them.

'There's nothing I can do!' Rot thought. 'Except...' he looked at the box attached to his halfway limb, 'I hope this does something...'

He pressed the red button.

A voice leapt out of the box, 'This is your favourite FM radio channel—Goa FM!'

Rot, of course, couldn't understand what the announcer was saying but he suddenly knew what the box was—a different version of the thing that had piped music into Reena's lab. He slapped his head. 'F' M radio! That was the 'F'!

The voice continued, 'And here's Goa's most popular rock band—*Band-width*!'

A loud, very loud, HORRENDOUSLY loud 'BABY, BABY, BABIIIEEE! YEAH, YEAH, YEAHHH!' exploded from the box and crashed through the pool. Sound becomes louder in water and this was teeth-rattlingly, bone-shakingly loud! Rot clapped his tentacles on his ears to keep from being deafened. So did Irrit and Po. Tumboo's flippers covered her ears in a trice.

'The whale!' Rot shouted. 'Look at the whale!'

Rakshus had stopped. The moment the 'music' had blasted out of the box, he had reared back as if punched in the nose. Now he grimaced and backed away, jerking, shaking. Whales have incredibly sensitive ears. They can hear sounds dozens of kilometres away. What was loud for Rot was shattering for the whale. And he had no protection! His fins were not long enough to cover his ears. 'BABY, BABY, BABIIIEEE' hammered on his eardrums, stomped on his brain, almost blew his eyes out of their sockets!

'Looks like he doesn't like rock!' Rot shouted, grinning.

'Must be a parent!' chuckled Tumboo.

Rakshus squealed in pain and raced away but 'YEAH, YEAH, YEAHHHH' followed him everywhere through the water. There was just one way out. Rakshus sped to the surface and leapt into the air!

CRACK! The sound of a gunshot rang around Sea World. Reena looked up from the sights of the tranquilizer gun at the soaring whale.

'Did you get him?' the Senior Supervisor asked.

'Yes,' Reena replied, watching the whale drop back into the water. 'It'll take a few minutes for the drug to work...'

There was a huge splash and Rakshus vanished underwater.

'Whoah!' Rot spluttered, toppling over from the

CRACK

force of the currents set off by the whale's splash.

The FM radio jerked loose from Rot's halfway limb and smashed into the pool wall before sinking to the floor. At once, the volume of the shrieks from the box dropped from 'unbearable' to merely 'annoying'.

'Uh-oh,' said Rot.

He shot a look at the whale. Rakshus, on the other side of the pool, stopped thrashing wildly and slowed down, looking confused.

'This is bad,' Rot muttered.

He picked up the box and shook it. The band kept wailing but this was irritating, not ear-splitting.

'What's the problem?' Tumboo asked.

'Trouble!' Rot replied.

'Boys!' Tumboo said. 'Can't do anything right!' She took the box from Rot and put her ear to it. 'Ow!' she said, jerking her head away. 'That's loud!'

'What?' Rot said. He grabbed the box, held it to his ear. 'Ouch!' he cried, instantly jerking away.

He spun around to look at the whale. With no nerve-rending sound to drive him mad, Rakshus had turned towards them, glaring, very, very angry. He looked from Irrit and Po to Rot and Tumboo, as if deciding whom to attack.

'Just one thing to do,' Rot said. 'Give me the claw, Tumboo.'

'Claw...' Tumboo muttered. 'Let's see...M...N...O...P...C! Here it is!'

'How can "C" come after N, O, P...forget it! Just give it here!'

Rot fastened the pouch to his halfway limb and swung it forward. The claw snapped open.

'What's the plan?' Tumboo asked.

'I'll have to jam the radio against the whale's ear,' Rot said. 'The claw's going to help me hold on!'

He sped away.

'H...hold on to the w...whale?' Tumboo stuttered. 'He...he's got water on the brain! Come back here right now, Rot!'

II

Rot raced towards the oncoming whale. Rakshus saw the octopus approach and opened his terrible jaws. Rot zoomed towards him and, at the last moment, vaulted over the gaping mouth, clamping on to the fin on the whale's back with the claw. Before the whale knew what was happening, Rot swung the box down and clapped it on to Rakshus' ear. 'BABY, BABY, BABIIIEEE' screamed into the whale's brain, bouncing back and forth in his skull.

Rakshus felt as if everything between his ears was on fire. He whimpered, rolled, jerked, thrashed, but he couldn't shake the horrible sound. Tumboo, Irrit and Po watched awestruck as the whale pitched and yawed, bucked and lurched through the pool. Rot had seen keepers ride dolphins and whales in Sea World shows but it had never been anything like this. Clamped to the whale's fin, Rot hung on desperately, holding the box firmly against Rakshus' ear. Rakshus started feeling numb all over. It was the sound, the awful sound! Then he remembered. For a few brief seconds when he had leapt into the air, the sound had vanished. He changed course and rocketed upward, launching his enormous body into the air.

'Shoot!' the Senior Super shrieked.

'Foot!' the Junior Super yelled.

Reena took aim at the leaping whale, tightened her finger on the trigger and…suddenly lowered the gun without having fired!

'What's wrong?' Dr Zwami demanded.

'The octopus! Look! Our octopus! He's riding the whale!'

'Wow!' Rot breathed, as he flew twenty feet into the air on the whale's back. 'What a view!'

The view, though spectacular, was the last thing on Rakshus' mind. There was no relief for Rakshus even out here in the open; he felt his strength drain away and he dropped like a chopped tree into the water.

Swimming fast (as turtles do), Tumboo hurried to the ladder. Irrit and Po were still stuck halfway up, too scared to move.

'Climb, you two no-good, lazy bums!' Tumboo yelled. 'Get your tentacles moving! Climb!'

Startled, Irrit and Po unwound their tentacles from the ladder's rungs. They started climbing, glancing fearfully at the struggling, staggering whale.

Rakshus could feel his senses go. Everything was darkening, his vision fading, his hearing growing weak. What a relief it was—he could barely hear that terrible shrieking sound. It wasn't crashing around in his skull, it wasn't burning his brain to a crisp. His mind had shrunk to contain just one thought—the last, deepest thought of a killer whale: to find its prey, to hunt, to kill. Through bleary eyes, Rakshus saw the octopuses climbing the ladder, a turtle in the water next to them. They had almost reached the surface. Silently, Rakshus rose. He twitched his tail feebly and lurched forward.

Rot didn't know quite what was happening. He had felt the whale's strength ebb, his struggles weaken. It was over, he had thought. But then the whale had risen, his fin (with Rot attached) breaking through the water surface. Rakshus was moving slowly, very slowly towards the ladder.

'Climb!' Tumboo yelled, seeing the whale heading towards them. 'Climb, you eight-legged blobs of goo!' she shouted at Irrit and Po. 'Climb!'

'Look at that!' Reena shouted, spotting Rot on the whale's back.

'H'een-credi-bull!' Dr Zwami exclaimed. 'The drug'z working, Dr Renaldo. The whale'z h'almozt knocked out!'

'A couple of minutes more. He's still got some...'

Suddenly, she saw Irrit and Po on the ladder. Rakshus was slowly, sluggishly making straight for them.

'Oh my god!' Reena cried. 'The octopuses! The whale's still after them!'

Inching forward, just a few feet from the octopuses and turtle, Rakshus opened his mouth wide. Irrit and Po gazed horrified at those awful teeth.

'He must have a real bad cough!' Tumboo said, looking down Rakshus' throat. 'Those are the biggest tonsils I've ever seen!'

On the whale's back, Rot was desperate. There were just moments left!

'What can I do?' he thought. 'What can I do?'

Nothing better occurred to him so he lifted the box he was holding against the whale's ear and smashed it down. If he were hoping to knock the whale out, he failed dismally. The box just bounced harmlessly off Rakshus's thick skull. Something did happen, however. The blow shook loose whatever had deadened the sound in the radio. Abruptly, a STUPENDOUSLY loud 'BABY, BABY, BABIIIEEE' exploded from the speaker. Rakshus jerked to a halt, his jaws went limp,

he seemed to moan and his eyes closed. He rolled right over and lay flat on his back. The whale was finally, completely knocked out.

'The whale'f unconfiouf!' the Junior Super shouted. 'H'EEN-credi-bull!'

'You did it, Dr Renaldo!'

'I didn't do a thing!' Reena said. 'The drug took too much time—the whale would have got the octopuses. It was our octopus who saved them, Dr Zwami, our wonderful, halfway-limbed octopus! Where is he?'

That's exactly what Tumboo was thinking. Where *was* Rot? The radio had floated to the surface, still merrily blasting out 'BABY, BABY, BABIIIEEE' but there was no sign of Rot. Was he all right? Tumboo had last seen him on the whale's back before Rakshus had rolled right over.

'Rot!' Tumboo called, worried. 'Rot!'

A tentacle emerged from the water and wrapped itself around the blaring box. Another tentacle followed and pressed the red button. 'BABY, BA...' the sound abruptly stopped. A grinning Rot popped out right behind.

'Rot, Rot, you're all right!' Tumboo shouted and

swam to him.

Rot waved to Reena who laughed and waved back. Then he turned to look at the unconscious Rakshus, fast asleep on his back.

Rot turned to Tumboo, grinning. 'He didn't even wait for the "Yeah, yeah, yeahhh"!'

It was two days later, but what a difference forty-eight hours can make! The sun was shining brightly and the spectators' galleries were packed with humans listening to the 'Final, Fanatastical Act' of the Sea World show—the oct-estra. Tumboo and Rot lay on a small outcropping of reef, watching Rot's brother Pyr swing it for the first time as a full-fledged member of the family group.

And when the music ended and the audience clapped and cheered and whistled, Rot felt his three octopus hearts swell with pride for Pyr.

'You know,' Rot said, 'I just realized something. Music doesn't hurt anymore!'

'I was thinking,' Tumboo said gently to Rot, 'you could easily get the lab lady to come up with a musical

attachment for your halfway limb. You could join the oct-estra, too.'

'I think we'll keep this stuff a secret between us, Tumbs,' Rot grinned. 'All superheroes have a secret identity! Like Batman...'

'...and Ms Robin!' Tumboo finished, chuckling and raising her flipper.

Laughing, the two friends high-one'd each other.